Five reasons why we think you'll love this book!

Winnie AND Wilbur

ENTURE

You get to see Winnie and Wilbur in fancy dress!

Contains treasure!

There is so much to spot in every picture.

This book has funny pirate words like 'hornswoggled' and 'blunderbuss'.

You can ta
how i

:hallenge:
unt?

Freya

Anushka

Maggie

Bailey

Johannes

Molly

Ashley

Amber

Jun-Yeong

Pablo

Matilda

Marwin

Hasan

Rebecca

Thank you to all these schools for helping
with the endpapers:

St Barnabas Primary School, Oxford; St Ebbe's Primary
School, Oxford; Marcham Primary School, Abingdon; St
Michael's C.E. Aided Primary School, Oxford; St Bede's
RC Primary School, Jarrow; The Western Academy,
Beijing, China; John King School, Pinxton; Neston
Primary School, Neston; Star of the Sea RC Primary
School, Whitley Bay; José Jorge Letria Primary School,
Cascais, Portugal; Dunmore Primary School, Abingdon;
Özel Bahçeşehir İlköğretim Okulu, Istanbul, Turkey; the
International School of Amsterdam, the Netherlands;
Princethorpe Infant School, Birmingham.

For Maxwell and Giann—V.T.

For James Watt who gave me my
first freelance job—K.P.

OXFORD
UNIVERSITY PRESS

Great Clarendon Street, Oxford OX2 6DP

Oxford University Press is a department of the University of Oxford.
It furthers the University's objective of excellence in research, scholarship,
and education by publishing worldwide. Oxford is a registered trade mark of
Oxford University Press in the UK and in certain other countries

Text copyright © Valerie Thomas 2013
Illustrations copyright © Korky Paul 2013, 2016
The moral rights of the author and artist have been asserted

Database right Oxford University Press (maker)

First published as *Winnie's Pirate Adventure* in 2013
This edition first published in 2016

British Library Cataloguing in Publication Data available

ISBN: 978-0-19-274818-8 (paperback)
ISBN: 978-0-19-274914-7 (paperback and CD)

10 9 8 7 6 5 4 3 2 1

Printed in China

Paper used in the production of this book is a natural, recyclable product made
from wood grown in sustainable forests. The manufacturing process conforms
to the environmental regulations of the country of origin

www.winnieandwilbur.com

VALERIE THOMAS AND KORKY PAUL

Winnie AND Wilbur

THE PIRATE ADVENTURE

OXFORD
UNIVERSITY PRESS

Winnie the Witch and her big black cat
Wilbur were getting ready for a party.
It was a fancy dress party to celebrate
Cousin Cuthbert's birthday.

'What will we wear, Wilbur?' asked Winnie.
'We'll have to think about that.'

Winnie thought
about it.

Cinderella?
No.

A bear?
No.

The Queen
of Hearts?
No, no!

Then Winnie had
a fantastic idea.

She waved her
magic wand,
shouted,
'Abracadabra!'

. . . and there she was, wearing a pirate costume.
Wilbur was in a parrot suit.

Winnie was pleased.
'We look fantastic!' she said.

Wilbur was embarrassed.

We look ridiculous,
he thought.

Winnie jumped onto her broomstick,
Wilbur jumped onto her shoulder,
and they flew off to the party.

There were some wonderful
costumes at the party.

Fairies, clowns, a lion, a princess,
some spacemen and *lots* of pirates.

Happy Birthday, Cuthbert!

The other pirates admired Winnie's parrot.
Wilbur flapped his wings.

'All we need now is a treasure map,' one pirate said.
'I found a treasure map in my pocket,'
said another pirate.
'So all we need now is a ship.'

'I can do that,' said Winnie.
She waved her magic wand, shouted,

'Abracadabra!'

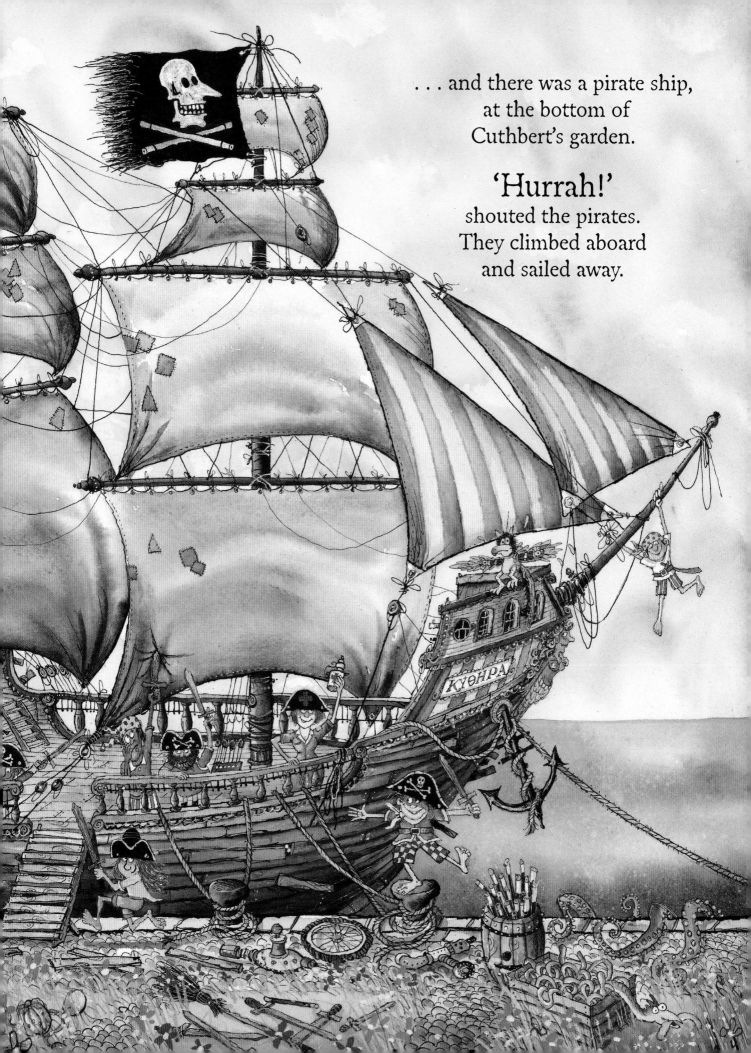

. . . and there was a pirate ship,
at the bottom of
Cuthbert's garden.

'Hurrah!'
shouted the pirates.
They climbed aboard
and sailed away.

'**Yo-ho-ho!**' shouted Winnie's pirates. 'Being a pirate is fun!'

They climbed up the masts.
They danced the hornpipe.
They walked the plank,
until Winnie fell in.

Luckily she could swim.

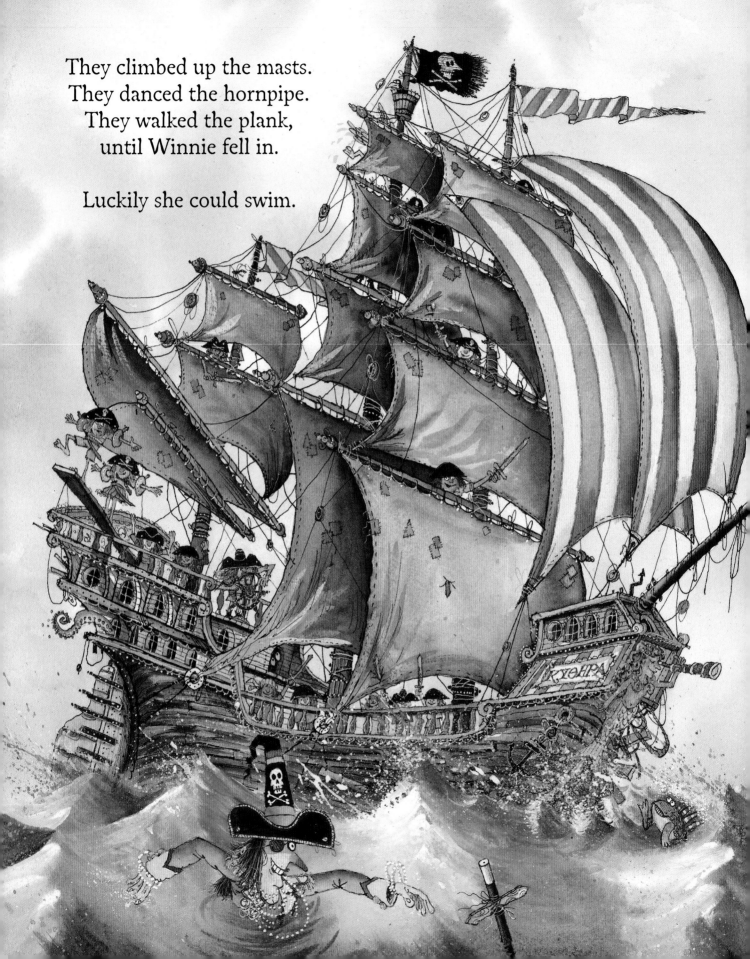

Wilbur climbed up to the crow's nest for a sleep,
but there was a crow inside.

'**Caw!**' said the crow.
She didn't want to share with a parrot.

Winnie's pirates got out the treasure map.
There were islands all around their ship.
Which one was the treasure island?

But then they saw an island
that looked exactly like the one
on the treasure map.

Winnie and her pirates splashed
ashore. They climbed to the top of a
hill and looked down.

There was another band of pirates digging up the treasure.
They had swords and daggers, cutlasses and blunderbusses.

They looked **fierce.**

'Will we stay and fight?' asked Winnie. 'Or go home?'

Winnie's pirates shouted . . .

'GO HOME!'

The real pirates looked up
and saw Winnie's pirates.

They ran back to their ship
with their swords and daggers,
their cutlasses and blunderbusses . . .

and sailed away.

Winnie's pirates were very surprised.

'Hurrah!' they shouted.
'We are fierce pirates!'

They ran down to the hole
in the sand and started digging.

It was hard work.

But at last they dug out the treasure chest.

Winnie lifted up the lid. The chest was empty.
'Shiver me timbers!' shouted Winnie's pirates.

'We've been hornswoggled!'

But Wilbur saw something
shining in the sand.

What was it?

He started to dig
and dig.

Out came a big shiny box.
And inside the box were lots
and lots of shiny tins . . . of sardines!

'Meee-yo-ho-ho!'
Wilbur was delighted. He loved sardines.

Winnie's pirates were not delighted.

But Winnie had a
wonderful idea.

She waved her wand,
shouted,

'Abracadabra!'

. . . and the
treasure chest
was full of
shiny treasure.

Now Winnie's pirates
were delighted.
They carried
the treasure and
Wilbur's sardines
back to the ship.

It was time to go home, but there was
no wind to blow their ship home again.

'I can fix that,' Winnie said.
She waved her magic wand,
and shouted, 'Abracadabra!'

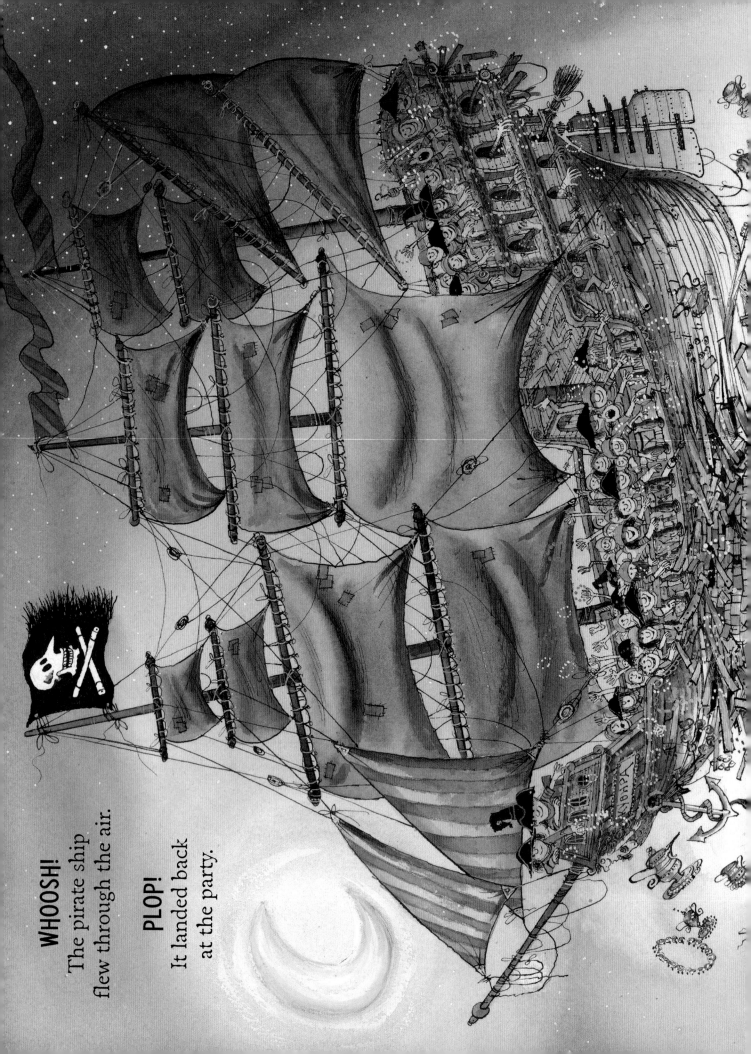

WHOOSH!
The pirate ship
flew through the air.

PLOP!
It landed back
at the party.

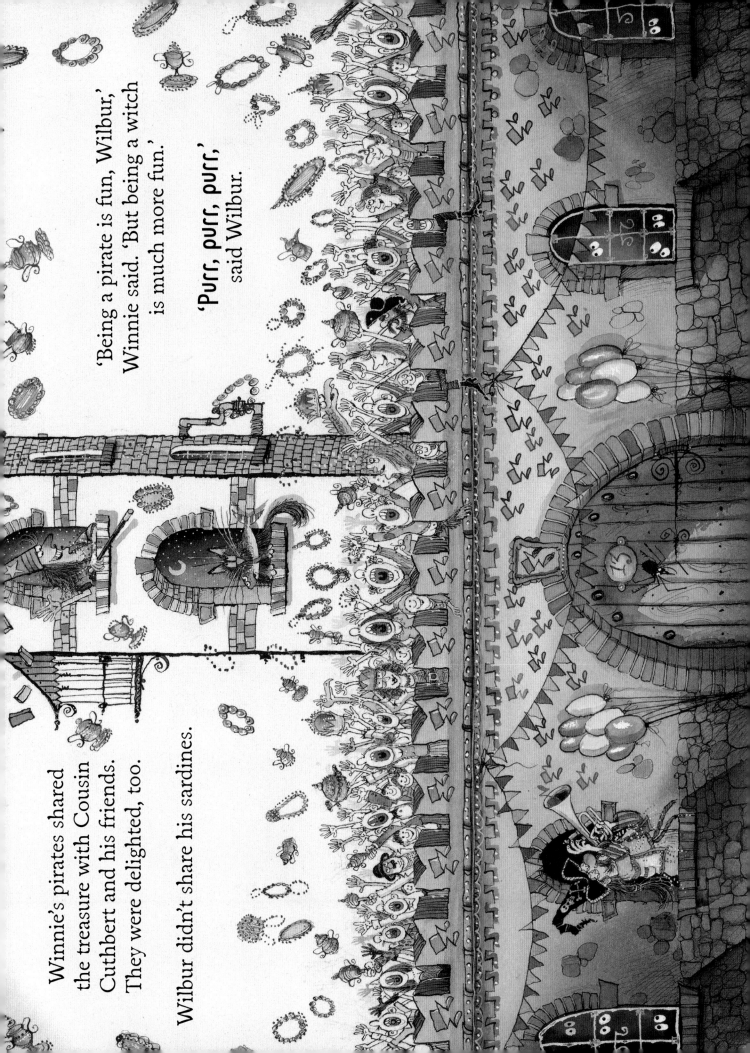

'Being a pirate is fun, Wilbur,'
Winnie said. 'But being a witch
is much more fun.'

'Purr, purr, purr,'
said Wilbur.

Winnie's pirates shared
the treasure with Cousin
Cuthbert and his friends.
They were delighted, too.

Wilbur didn't share his sardines.

Bethany

Katia

Eun-Jae

Kathleen

Ji-Eun

Jenny

Sara

Fraser

Ka Keung

Selin

Selin

Olivia

Siyabend

Kieran

A note for grown-ups

Oxford Owl is a FREE and easy-to-use website packed with support and advice about everything to do with reading.

Informative videos

Hints, tips and fun activities

Top tips from top writers for reading with your child

Help with choosing picture books

For this expert advice and much, much more about how children learn to read and how to keep them reading ...

LO,OK
for Oxford Owl
www.oxfordowl.co.uk